Black Lives Matter
Poetry

Devajit Bhuyan

Ukiyoto Publishing

All global publishing rights are held by

Ukiyoto Publishing

Published in 2023

Content Copyright © Devajit Bhuyan

ISBN 9789360169404

All rights reserved.
No part of this publication may be reproduced, transmitted, or stored in a retrieval system, in any form by any means, electronic, mechanical, photocopying, recording or otherwise, without the prior permission of the publisher.

The moral rights of the author have been asserted.

This book is sold subject to the condition that it shall not by way of trade or otherwise, be lent, resold, hired out or otherwise circulated, without the publisher's prior consent, in any form of binding or cover other than that in which it is published.

www.ukiyoto.com

Dedicated to my beloved wife Late Mitali Bhuyan, my inspiration to write poetry. Miss you Mitali.

Contents

Black Lives Matter	1
Racist Are Enemy Of Humanity	2
Racial Discrimination Must Pack	3
Racism Is Genetic	4
Colour Of Skin Is Only Like A Gown	5
Colour Of Skin Not A Choice	6
Racial Discrimination Is Sin	7
Reboot American Society	8
Americans, Protest Peacefully	9
Corona Is Not Racial	10
Civilization Has Not Moved Ahead	11
For Division Reasons Are Multiple	12
American Green Card Is Your Crown	13
Suicide	14
When You Commit Suicide	15
Suicide Is Never A Solution	16
Suicide Is End Point Of Depression	17
Suicide Is Not A Matter To Be Glorified	18
Suppression	19
War Is Not Solution	20
Prophets Said	21
How, Why, What?	22
Farewell To Corona	23
PPE Kit	24
Corona Proof Jacket	25
Scientists Please Find Why And How	26
Invisible Enemy Is Dangerous	27
Quarantine	28

Corona Said	29
Cough	30
Corona Virus Will Stay	31
Let Corona Bark	32
Think For Paradigm Shift	33
Change Is For Better	34
Break The Chain	35
O' God Please Forgive Us	36
Fear Is The Change Agent	37
Redefine Progress	38
Health Care Priority First	39
Economic Package Is Not Remedy	40
Citizens Want To Open Door	41
Corona Forced To Lift The Veil	42
The Big Picture	43
Mother Earth Is Severely Ill	44
When We Repent And Cry	45
When Solution Is Not In Our Hand	46
Best Donation	47
Donate Your Eye After Death	48
Work From Home	49
Mystery Of Life	50
Boredom	51
Be Like Electricity	52
Environment Day	53
Celebration Of Environment Day Not Enough	54
Cadet	55
Caesar's Wife	56
Breakup	57
In Mother In Law's Grip	58

Don't Be Ashamed Of Depression	59
Lifestyle Will Change	60
Book Should Not Be Like Floppy	61
Always Try To Be Kind	62
Make Everyday A Good Day	63
Beyond Imagination	64
Remember Also For Father	65
Containment	66
Run	67
Attention	68
Life Is Uncertain Than Cricket	69
Need And Greed	70
Solar Eclipse	71
Sun Is The Heart	72
You Don't Know My Friend	73
Mind	74
Why We Are Here?	75
We Come For Limited Time	76
Go To Planetarium	77
Father's Day	78
Be Grateful	79
Friends Are Also Teacher	80
Learning	81
Man Is Pushed Back	82
Sleep	83
Welcome To Garden	84
Behind The Naughty Smile	85
Transmission	86
Love Is Blind	87
Dalai Lama	88

Why Me?	89
Salute The Indian Hero	90
Marriage	91
Wife	92
Regret	93
I Don't Want A Life Living On Pill	94
No One Remain Young Forever	95
When A Puzzle We Can't Solve	96
Whom Should We Blame?	97
No Point For The Past To Regret	98
I Pray For Your Good Health	99
The Human Civilization Has Resilience	100
Human Civilization Will Not Accept Defeat	101
Salute Mothers On Mother's Day	102
Sometimes We Become Lonely Sailor	103
Might Is Always Not Right	104
Crazy People	105
I Am No More Hero	106
Misery Of The Poor	107
Eat Without Mouth	108
Poetry Is Free Flow	109
Think Global Act Local	110
Only For Human Situation Is Critical	111
For Better Life People Migrate	112
March Ahead	113
Electricity Can't Be Seen	114
Electrical Is At Top	115
Migrant Workers	116
Come Out Smiling	117
Human Supremacy Nullified	118

Budget	119
Don't Demotivate Frontline Warrior	120
Whom To Be Saluted?	121
What Next?	122
Night Is Now Night	123
Newspapers Are In Trouble	124
VC (Video Conferencing)	125
Don't Be Afraid	126
He Who Afraid Is Dead	127
How To Save Economy?	128
Life And Economy Both Are In Danger	129
No Need To Make Life Slow	130
New Generation, Don't Worry	131
Body Language	132
Middle Class Has Become Lonely	133
Swab Test	134
Enemy Of Poor	135
We Are Helpless	136
The Virtual World	137
Fear Of Death	138
Epidemic	139
World Is Burning	140
Life Has Become Dull	141
Don't Worry, Be Happy	142
Good News Coming Soon	143
Astrology	144
Religion Need Substitution	145
Politics	146
Religion And Politics	147
Don't Hate Sinner	148

Pain	149
Cave Man	150
Baba Ramdev	151
Someone May Be Rowdy	152
Failure And Suicide	153
Sour To Sweet Always Matter	154
Toe To Top	155
Truth Is Always Truth	156
We Pray Sun And Moon	157
Saturday Night Fever	158
Bad Potato	159
Religion Is Deep Rooted	160
Peace	161
Career And Opportunity	162
Career And Life	163
We Are Good In Corruption	164
Luxury Cruise	165
Street Vendor	166
Happiness Is Like Morning Dew	167
Failed Marriages	168
Cyber Crime	169
What My Poems Mean	170
Simplicity	171
Defeat Is Never Final	172
Good Morning	173
Gravity	174
No One Will Share Your Pain	175
The Dust	176
Use Your Money	177
Thoughts	178

India-China Standoff	179
Snake	180
Don't Carry Painful Burden	181
China, Enjoy Your Own Territory	182
Decision Making	183
Broker	184
China Is Destabilising World	185
No One Can Stop Time	186
Green	187
Luck	188
Obedience	189
Teacher Teaches	190
Lecture	191
Dependency	192
Innovation	193
Age Is Gift Of Time	194
Animal Sacrifice Is Superstition	195
Untold Agony	196
Kick	197
Evil	198
Today Is The Right Time	199
Today Or Never	200
All Lives Matter	201
Make Democracy Better	202
For Better World	203
Cleanliness	204
If You Live In Poverty	205
Bamboo	206
Give And Take	207
The World Is Whole, Perfect And Complete	208

Poverty And Discrimination	209
Master And Slave	210
Pseudo Religious	211
Woman	212
How To Avoid Depression	213
Healing	214
Blame	215
All Well If Ends Well	216
Surname	217
Follow Safety Measures Seriously	218
Farmers Can't Work From Home	219
Farmer's, Please Work Online	220
Season Is Changing As Usual	221
Faith	222
We Have Destroyed Elephant's Habitat	223
O' My Miser Friend	224
We Must Kill The Bustard Corona	225
Purpose Of Life	226
Love For Children Is A Binding Force	227
Faith	228
Go To Garden And Shout	229
I Am Nothing	230
Einstein	231
Block	232
Silver Lining	233
Nothing Is In Our Hand	234
What Is God	235
Grace Of God	236
The Cruellest Animal	237
Inequalities	238

Gender Discrimination	239
I Am Insignificant	240
Hypocrisy	241
I Love Jesus And Buddha	242
About the Author	*243*

Black Lives Matter

Black lives matter
Let us make this world better
We must make human values greater
Civilization will then move higher
In rainbow all colours are together.
All human beings have same hunger
Black, white, brown drink same water
To humanity racism is deadly thunder
Killing in the name of colour is blunder
We have to say goodbye racism forever.
Black lives equally matter
Greeting them with smile is smarter
This will make your life wider
The journey of life will be easier
Relationships are hidden treasure.
People whom you ignore may be important
In future he may become most significant
The smile you gave to him will come back
His heart, your smile will easily hack
Always smile to people for return gift pack.

Racist Are Enemy Of Humanity

Who encourage racism are shameless
Their existence as human is useless
Though man, they are always heartless
Their education and knowledge baseless
One day they will leave world nameless.
Racism is against teaching of Christianity
Racist people are man without integrity
They are the worst enemy of humanity
To fight against racism is everyone's duty
No nation should allow racism in their jetty.

Racial Discrimination Must Pack

Racism is in some people's gene
To continue racism, they are keen
Possibility of change is very thin
Sometimes racism becomes lean
A small incident makes it green
Ego of white supremacy is fake
Change of mind they must make
On their ego mankind must press break
New attitude white must take
Soon racial discrimination must pack.

Racism Is Genetic

Racism is a disease genetic
In history it was never static
Even in tribal life it was basic
Relations of tribes not harmonic
Caste, creed also has racial logic
Colour of skin is a big divisive force
Look of face is also a racists source
New hybrid generation can only reduce
Scientists, please new gene try to produce
Racism free new people in world introduce.

Colour Of Skin Is Only Like A Gown

Man, maybe white, black or brown
But same type of brain is their crown
Red blood is in every body's town
Without heart everyone will be down
Colour of skin is only like a gown
All colours need air, water and food
Discrimination for colour is not good
Black and white two sides of the coin
Without both, life in world can't join
Matters can't exist only with one ion.

Colour Of Skin Not A Choice

Colour of skin is not a matter of choice
But you can make beautiful your voice
Colour is because of nature's random dice
Discrimination in the name of colour is vice
Like black, white people also eat wheat and rice
Geography and environment made the difference
In cold weather white people got preference
In hot and humid conditions black better preference
Eyes may be blue, black, brown, golden or red
With same materials, chromosome all is made.

Racial Discrimination Is Sin

Christianity don't encourage discrimination
Jesus gave his life for human integration
Caste, creed, colour etc are false division
Racial discrimination is the biggest sin
To eradicate it, Jesus would have been keen
One world, one human race should be the goal
All human lives matter is the humanity's call
If racial discrimination continue, humanity will fall
Against racism let us build a wall thick and tall
One day no one will enter the racists ugly hall.

Reboot American Society

Death of a person in police custody is painful
But rioting in the name of protest is shameful
Why are you destroying property of innocent?
They are in no way related to the killing incident
Protest, but to law of the land always be obedient
The world doesn't deserve violence in the largest democracy
Large scale mob lynching will encourage support for autocracy
The pride of civil liberty will be tainted by looting
American must go for new movement for social rebooting
Otherwise, division in American society will be everlasting.

Americans, Protest Peacefully

Everyone has right to peaceful protest
But no one is authorised to create unrest
Protest through nonviolence path is best
For protesters keeping peace is the test
Otherwise, protest should be given rest
Neither all blacks are innocent and good
Nor all white people are cruel and rude
It depends on upbringing and attitude
In both colours there are lots of prostitute
Colour don't determine degree of gratitude.

Corona Is Not Racial

In America also, Corona is not racial
To black and white treatment is equal
The internet and social media are practical
Social discrimination is a disease global
Why man can't, learn and be true social?
Racial discrimination is part of civilization
It has no place in the era of computerization
People should go for attitude modernisation
To chase racism, change of mindset is only solution
Till then racism free world will remain as an illusion.

Civilization Has Not Moved Ahead

Civilization has not moved ahead
Only older technology become dead
Our mindset is still in mediaeval age
We are bounded in the religious cage
Mediaeval teachings are in front page
We use technology to promote falsehood
For irrational religious texts always stood
Technology is not used to modernize mood
For us every religious verse is true and good
Modern lifestyle failed to change our attitude.

For Division Reasons Are Multiple

Religion can easily divide people
Colour of skin is also reason simple
For division reasons are in multiple
Divisive forces grow quickly like pimple
But blood flow in red colour is humble
Air, water, light and time never divide
Platform of unity only always provide
All the discriminations are man made
To divide man nature have never said
Even in twenty first century it has not fade.

American Green Card Is Your Crown

Colour may be black, red or brown
The American green card is your crown
Now why destroy your own town?
You are crazy for the American passport
For destruction of America why support?
To work for America, you are import
For destruction you may get deport
Unity and integrity of America is important
Stray incident doesn't support destruction
You must pay for the reconstruction.

Suicide

Depression alone can't compel suicide
Reason must be poisonous like cyanide
To vent pain, window to mind provide
With friends and dear one tragedy divide
Look to underprivileged, depression will subside
Suicide is not simply a medical condition
Medicines alone can't provide restriction
Body, mind, soul need perfect coordination
With medicine, meditation is good combination
Control suicidal thoughts with determination.

When You Commit Suicide

When you commit suicide
Out of emotion you decide
If you talk, emotion will recede
Friends will stand beside
Allow parents to preside
Suicide put family into pain
Whole life, for them tragedy remain
Through suicide no one gain
Your beloved, why you slain?
To your mind confidence you train.

Suicide Is Never A Solution

Suicide is never the solution
It is only escaping dilution
It is the worst way to face situation
Better wait and watch from hibernation
Time will give you good resolution
Pain maybe too heavy to bear and carry
Struggle forced you to forget being merry
Yet drive on your fully loaded lorry
Enjoy on road eating wild black berry
To suicide immediately say sorry.

Suicide Is End Point Of Depression

Suicide is end point of depression

Dangerous is continued suppression

With friends do its compression

Games, sports, travelling are also solution

Suicide push parents to humiliation

Our life is not for ourselves alone

We are our parent's future backbone

Our suicide will make them lifeless stone

They will be forced to the depression zone

Consult doctor to control depressive hormone.

Suicide Is Not A Matter To Be Glorified

Suicide is not a matter to be glorified
Some killed himself being dissatisfied
His action need not to be simplified
After his death nothing can be rectified
Killing is not a good issue to be dignified
Attempt to suicide is attempted to murder
The person needs counselling for blunder
Ending one's own life is not very easy
He who committed suicide must be crazy
In the matter of committing suicide be lazy.

Suppression

Suppression can't create impression
It can't also remove depression
Suppression is never a solution
For problem it is not substitution
It only gives temporary dilution
Suppression of weak is not at all fair
Better sorrow of underprivileged share
Brotherhood through suppression is rare
Suppression will not encourage love and care
It will create in mind a dirty irrelevant layer.

War Is Not Solution

War is not the solution of dispute
Negotiation is best resolving route
High level teams India, China depute
Silk route friendship is of age-old repute
Peaceful resolution world will salute
The world is now fighting an epidemic
Hostility at this time will not be democratic
India, China both have nuclear weapon
For world war a small spark may be reason
To save humanity find negotiated solution.

Prophets Said

Prophets said that all lives in earth matter
Even dog, fox, donkey is also our brother
Their souls are also part of same Father
Cruelty to living creature is crime and sin
God's blessings cruel man can never win
Every human life in the world is precious
Discrimination for colour is offence serious
Racist people are criminals notorious
For the mankind they are dangerous

How, Why, What?

How long we will go on sanitising?
How long we will go on criticising?
How long we have to avoid socialising?
How long it will take for rationalizing?
How long it will take for customizing?
Why nature, forced social distancing?
Why nature, infect without discriminating?
Why nature, whole world contaminating?
Why nature, closed normal life maintaining?
Why nature says, no more animal hunting?
What is the reason behind all happening?
What is the reason of Corona boiling?
What is the reason for human killing?
What is the reason nature is nailing?
What is the reason vaccine is failing?
The answers to how, why, what must come
Permanent solutions to the Covid19 must be done.

Farewell To Corona

The farewell to Corona shall be grand
Unique will be the departing band
Every man will clap and stand
People will hug their good friend
In lifestyle there will be smiling trend
Corona will say goodbye mankind
Better meaning of life please find
To the nature always be kind
I came for the purpose to remind
The lesson you have learned keep in mind.

PPE Kit

With PPE kit Doctors are fit
Without it, Corona they meet
Day and night, they treat
Majority patients are now fit
Even in supplying kit, China cheat
Wearing kit for long is difficult
Breathless situation may result
Yet medical staff must wear
Now they are society's very dear
For their services, let us cheer.

Corona Proof Jacket

PPE kit is Corona proof jacket
Corona can't enter in nurse's basket
Bullet proof jackets are for soldiers
The kit is for the Corona warriors
The virus can't penetrate its barriers
Masks, gloves, sanitizer all are handy
But wearing PPE kit is not at all trendy
After wearing it no one can eat even candy
The kit is frontline weapon in Corona war
It is now precious than bullet proof car.

Scientists Please Find Why And How

Scientists, please do root cause analysis
Temporary measure is now dialysis
Symptomatic treatment can't resolve crisis
We need more and more research thesis
The whole gambit should be the basis;
Why and how the virus came we must know
It is not enough if we simply stop its rapid flow
In future anywhere, any moment it will again grow
More dangerous may be the destructive show
Scientists please quickly find why and how.

Invisible Enemy Is Dangerous

Invisible enemy is dangerous
To face them be serious
The fight is always tedious
Action can't be spontaneous
You can't see the notorious
Any moment they can be furious
Staying near can be injurious
Cohabiting may be ridiculous
No need of relation harmonious
Save your life, it is precious.

Quarantine

I am not afraid of the virus
But I am afraid of the circus
The ring will be my radius
About me all will discuss
To my family people will be bias
Quarantine is fearsome than the disease
Tension and depression it will increase
Neighbour will fearfully look after release
No one likes in society troll and tease
Everyone now suspects if you are Chinese.

Corona Said

Corona said
Trap laid
Masks made
We paid
Police raid;
Covid19 unstoppable
Life become vulnerable
Economy now unstable
Fear is palpable
Stay inside, be humble.

Cough

In the world, once upon a time
I was considered to be fine
With me people used to dine
No restrictions from friends to wine
But now everyone afraid of mine;
Still I am a normal disease
Helped doctors to earn fees
But now even doctors are afraid of me
Now no one anywhere want to see
The Covid19 forced me to flee.

Corona Virus Will Stay

Corona virus will stay
But will be aloof like gay
People will talk and say
Will try to avoid in the day
For protection ready to pay;
We must live with the Covid19 virus
There will be no more lockdown curious
To protect own life people will be serious
Attitude to stranger will not be harmonious
For social life the damage is tremendous.

Let Corona Bark

We are too close to vaccine
Soon will come curable medicine
The Covid19 episode will be memory
People will tell children the story
Some will cry remembering history;
So, don't be afraid and act in panic
In loneliness enjoy the beauty scenic
The world has become a beautiful park
Don't roam thinking future may be dark
Enjoy life and move ahead, let Corona bark.

Think For Paradigm Shift

Corona has entered a new phase
To face it let us build different stage
We must come out of self-made cage
The virus is going to stay indefinite days
Open the door to come beautiful rays;
Let's think for paradigm shift in strategy
If we don't change there will be big tragedy
Soon world will see largescale malnutrition
Lockdown can't be a permanent solution
Need of the hour is fear psychosis dilution.

Change Is For Better

Change is always for better
People have become smarter
Corona act as the starter
Lockdown pushed later
Better tomorrow always matter
Change has happened for good
People are busy searching food
To destroy environment no mood
To weaker animals not at all rude
Cheaper become oil and crude.

Break The Chain

Break the chain
World will gain
Lesser will be pain
To prevent is main
Virus will go to drain
Children we must train
Efforts will not go in vain
Soon there will be rain
Corona will not come again
Let us together break the chain.

O' God Please Forgive Us

We are sailing in a ship without a rudder
O' Lord show us the direction like father
Corona is torturing us with its hunter
People are queuing in hospital counter
World is now suffering for China's blunder;
The hole on the bottom is becoming larger
Every day increasing the sinking danger
Doctors are fighting with crossed finger
People in the ship is suffering from hunger
Please forgive us for our sin and blunder.

Fear Is The Change Agent

This beautiful world Corona can't change
The fear in human minds is reason main
If fears subside, the world will look same
Lockdown, fear all is created by our brain
Experts said that we have to break the chain
The death of innocent people has pained
Yet, for all these activities environment gained
Ecological balance has cheerfully sustained
To face disaster, the young generation is trained
One day Corona will also be firmly chained.

Redefine Progress

Time to redefine human progress
Fast car and high-rise alone not success
Pure water and air is more important
Ecological balance is very pertinent
For better life biodiversity is supplement;
Development does not mean shopping mall
We have seen how quickly it can fall
Better health care must be available to all
No need of skyscrapers and towers tall
Cycle of human life's domain is very small.

Health Care Priority First

Food, shelter and clothes must
Health care is priority first
Information technology give trust
Environment should not be allowed to rust
Otherwise human civilization will burst;
No need of so-called progress fast
Let the value system in society last
A tiny virus can make civilization past
So now forget your greed and lust
Saving humanity is our duty just.

Economic Package Is Not Remedy

Economic package is not remedy
It is only a temporary comedy
Soon the vaccine should be ready
Otherwise life will remain cloudy
There will be no more party goody-goody;
If Corona continues to remain proudly
Even bold and beautiful can't shout loudly
No one will be able to hug and kiss fondly
Emotions and attitudes will suffer badly
Relationships in the society will be deadly.

Citizens Want To Open Door

Nights are coming with curfew
Everyday leaders are doing review
Before them no previous preview
No one has any clear-cut view
What experts tell, leader has to chew;
Lockdown one, two, three and four
Till now this could not touch the core
Experts will ask for lockdown more
Staying inside home people became bore
Citizens now want to open their door.

Corona Forced To Lift The Veil

Neither Trump nor Jinping nor Modi can decide future
In the world now Covid19 is the de-facto master
The world economy is helpless to Corona hunter
Self-goal in the fight against virus is a big blunder
Lockdown without remedial measures is only surrender;
Life is precious every human being know well
In the name of saving lives millions pushed to hell
Everyone now realised mistakes and ringing the bell
Bailout packages worldwide now at discount sale
From lockdown Corona himself forced to lift the veil.

The Big Picture

Corona is now the picture
The name itself is torture
Emerges a stay home culture
Social life is under pressure
Get together totally puncture;
Time has come to think beyond
The social life must rebound
In parties we should hear sound
Children should play around
Cheers must return to Olympic ground.

Mother Earth Is Severely Ill

Mother earth is severely ill
So is Corona's nonstop kill
Skyrocketing medical bill
Not available curing pill
Lockdown is only mock drill;
Mother earth we have to cure
Covid19 will go out be sure
To teach us a lesson it's tenure
Environment must become pure
Covid19 should be reason to lure.

When We Repent And Cry

When we repent and cry
Hate of our mind becomes dry
God never remains shy
To help us God sincerely try
The evils can't make our fry;
When we are free from greed
Limited becomes our need
To our prayers God always heed
With generosity God feed
Towards fulfilment he led.

When Solution Is Not In Our Hand

When solution is not in our hand
When fear and uncertainty is the trend
Pray God to become your friend
Ray of light and hope he will send
The road ahead will take a sharp bend;
The problem may be hard and tough
At your falling people may laugh
But to prayer God never behave rough
Solution will come for fever and cough
Infront of God, the devil can't bluff.

Best Donation

No donation is better than eye donation
You have no use of eyes after cremation
Doctor can preserve it with your permission
For someone it will give lifetime solution
You can see the world with determination
To donate eyes, you need a brave heart
It will prove that you are kind and smart
A journey even after death you will start
After leaving world you will be its part
Let's donate eye to fill someone's cart.

Donate Your Eye After Death

Eyes may be black, blue, golden or brown
It is human life's most precious crown
Without eyes, forever human life is down
You can't see beauty of nature and town
Blind people can't feel colour of own gown
Without eyes, light is of no use
The rainbow can never amuse
Can't realise that elephant is huge
Thank God the best crown can be reuse
Donate your eye, it will be good news.

Work From Home

From home the barber can't cut hair
To the farmers the call is not fair
Without movement delivery is rare
All human works robots can't share
Doctors can't take critical patients care;
Work from home is only for limited people
For the working class it is not so simple
With job loss and hunger they are humble
The drivers and porters heard it as ripple
Work from home is tougher than dribble.

Mystery Of Life

Impossible to understand mystery of life
Equally difficult to understand wife
Life and death are separated by a dotted line
Any moment you can see cloud or sunshine
So, better to accept everything is normal and fine
No one knows how mystery of life will unfold
Many things in life always remain untold
The memories in mind, only you can hold
The better way to face the misery is to be bold
Till death takes you to the graveyard's fold.

Boredom

World population is suffering from boredom
Work and movement can't be done random
In Niagara Falls you will see tourists seldom
Whole world is now Corona's own fiefdom
The virus is invading mankind in random
Maintaining distance is boring job
O' God our freedom in twenty-twenty why you rob
Please unlock from world the Corona knob
America is destroyed by unruly criminals and mob
By any means, from world of boredom we have to lob.

Be Like Electricity

Be efficient like electric motor
Move continuously like rotor
Become static like a transformer
Transform life in the society forever
Be active like a transmitter
Always send message for better
Be bright like a LED light
With minimum make life bright
Be invisible like electricity
Work always without publicity.

Environment Day

To save environment should be attitude
To mother nature it will be gratitude
Protection requires bigger magnitude
Start a battle to preserve beloved solitude
Propagate the message to far off latitude
World Environment Day is symbolic reminder
By destroying environment, we have done blunder
Unabated felling of tree will push mankind to danger
The challenges ahead are much bigger
By planting trees let us make our future better.

Celebration Of Environment Day Not Enough

Celebration alone is not enough
If we are not serious, time will laugh
Environmental law should be tough
No one should be allowed to do rough
Already destruction done is enough
The dynamic equilibrium must be saved
Environment's enemy should be caged
Development should be eco-friendly based
Your protest voice must be strongly raised
The destroyer should forever be chased.

Cadet

Left right, left right
Make your life bright
Don't take discipline light
On training, show your might
In difficult field bravely fight
Training is tough and tight
With ease, you can climb height
You never lose your sight
Many a times sleepless night
You work to remove nation's plight.

Caesar's Wife

Always must be above suspicion
Being Caesar's wife is a distinction
Must support to find best solution
Sometimes you may face humiliation
Should not allow authority dilution
Caesar's wife backbone of power circle
She should always smile with dimple
Even with lot of power she must be bumble
In minor pressure she should not buckle
To become Caesar's wife is tough, not simple.

Breakup

In relationships breakup is painful
But breakup is not at all shameful
The jealous people become cheerful
In relationships some people are harmful
Some people enjoy when eyes are tearful
Before you breakup first try to makeup
Small old matters don't try to wakeup
When other people poke, say shut up
To compromise always warmup
Before you breakup, the dispute hush up.

In Mother In Law's Grip

If you are in grips of mother-in-law
You will certainly enter in debts jaw
Expenses will come one by one in row
You will lose your face's beautiful glow
You can't defy because to wife you vow
Soon your finance and liquidity will be low
The burden life you will be unable to tow
But wife and mother-in-law will cheer wow
They will never let you to go slow
To lenders you will have to bow.

Don't Be Ashamed Of Depression

Like hate, anger, joy is also depression
Always it is not a negative emotion
But it should be kept under compression
Drugs and medicine alone are not solution
Use of drugs should not become addiction
Reading and creative work is the solution
Make creativity your all-time companion
Sometimes drugs may be needed for dilution
But don't use it all the time for hibernation
To overcome depression, you need determination.

Lifestyle Will Change

Lifestyle of people will change
People will walk in different range
Resources they will better manage
Man will work to reduce wastage
Will be happy with light luggage
People will be fond of travelling wild
In jungle fear of contamination is mild
Parents will play hide and seek with child
Social distancing will force avoid party
Moving alone, people will avoid places dirty.

Book Should Not Be Like Floppy

Book should not become like floppy
Its journey is now very, very sloppy
In market we can sell limited copy
To save from rain we are putting canopy
Can book comeback winning the trophy
Responsibility is now with the reader
There is no dearth of good writer
Also, easy to get a self-publishing publisher
But getting the readers is the barrier
Will people support to make book winner?

Always Try To Be Kind

Always don't remain same my mind
Sometimes it becomes unkind
To others misery it remains blind
Selfish way very easily it can find
For own survival in box, it is bind
At times mind becomes very kind
Generosity it loves to freely unwind
All misery goes with cool wind
Because mind realise life will end
So, to mind good thoughts always send.

Make Everyday A Good Day

We can make our everyday good
Enjoy always vegetarian food
Eat nonveg only to change mood
No day come to us to make life rude
Every day sun comes pure and nude
Tomorrow will certainly be better
Today's food will make you fatter
Realise that today is important matter
Never push the good moment to later
Make today a memorable day rather.

Beyond Imagination

We must adjust for cohabitation
Already started social transmission
Always can't stay in isolation
Only weapon to take precaution
Frequently do hand sensitization
Lockdown is not permanent solution
It can only do temporary dilution
The virus is doing continuous evolution
People eagerly waiting for vaccination
But when vaccine comes beyond imagination.

Remember Also For Father

When you love your mother
Remember also for father
They make you champion together
Love for mom is always higher
If you love equally, it is better
Father may be rough and tough
Yet, in his heart love is always enough
At your silly jokes he may not laugh
But for your joy, money he will cough
To save you in danger, he will never bluff.

Containment

For our safety is zone containment
In life also containment is very pertinent
Money and wealth alone are not supplement
In life if you have minimum requirement
We always realise it only after retirement
Containment can give in life satisfaction
Greed can never be life's good resolution
To many problems, containment is solution
It is also the path for your need dilution
Containment helps to overcome worst situation.

Run

Run, run and run
Work with fun
For safety carry gun
When hungry eat bun
For light, thank sun;
Respect the nun
Work hard to earn
If required, take a turn
From other people learn
But to win run and run.

Attention

When you give attention
You can find a solution
Attention helps in rectification
Attention also gives resolution
Never push it to hibernation
Attention is needed in classroom
With attention result will boom
Without attention the flower doesn't bloom
You can't even clean floor with the broom
If you drive without attention, life is doom.

Life Is Uncertain Than Cricket

Life is more uncertain than cricket
In bathroom may fall your wicket
No one can claim, he will hit century
Time will prove it to be a perjury
Tomorrow may write his obituary
In the uncertainty lies beauty of life
We are duty bound to love our wife
Any moment she may give a bouncer
To entertain he have to become a jocker
Next, if you don't face googly, you are luckier.

Need And Greed

If you can't differentiate need and greed
Your whole life will unhappily proceed
In gathering wealth, you may succeed
But love and affection will be diminished
Chasing mirage, one day you will be finished
Need and greed try to distinguish every day
With a smile to the waiter tips happily pay
Put some money on the baggers tray
To swim in the sea no need to buy a bay
Without your greed sun will always give ray.

Solar Eclipse

Natural phenomenon is an eclipse
Superstition has no scientific basis
Sun will move in its orbit as usual
Towards solar eclipse be casual
But don't look at the sun, be careful
The Indian demons Rahu, Ketu are myth
No planet will ever change rotating path
Planetary position is not going to harm
In planetarium enjoy eclipse's charm
Ignore all astrologers false beat of drum.

Sun Is The Heart

In solar system, sun is heart and soul
Eclipse is momentary situation, not foul
It happens in the system in cyclical order
For bad effects of eclipse do not bother
Only request is to take care of earth mother
All planets in the system are delicately balanced
The planetary movement is perfectly maintained
The centre stage, the sun always retained
The shadow of planets and satellites is natural
Physics has explained planetary movement well.

You Don't Know My Friend

You don't know my friend
How much pain I am carrying,
Yet in the darkest night
I dream for the full moon
In the black clouds
I search the rainbow
When there is thunder storm
I look for the petals of rose
Even if there is hurdles of hills
I continue to flow like spring
When the dearest one break my heart
I allow them to fly and become smart
I am keeping all my pain
In the deepest corner of heart
If carbon can become diamond under pressure
My pain will also bloom like heavenly flower.

Mind

Nothing is more negative than the mind
Every step fault it can easily find
It can break years of friendship
For a flimsy or silly reason
For hate it can go for treason
It can start a quarrel with a smile
It can instigate to kill within a while
Mind can be cruel than the butcher
In killing sacrificial goat always smarter
Negativity is the creation of sick mind
It's remedy inside your mind can only be find.

Why We Are Here?

If our birth is without any reason
The world for us is a prison
Everything will be fair and just
No value of the word called trust
Only survival is must
Honesty, integrity everything will rust
No need of justice and fair play
We can do whatever we say
For our existence reason may whatsoever
With love and brotherhood let's bind together.

We Come For Limited Time

We come to this world for a limited time
So, we should always try to make it fine
For survival in the world, we must dine
To enjoy with friends sometimes wine
The land I have bought is forever not mine
Nobody knows how long he will live
So, if you have, don't hesitate to give
Tomorrow morning you may not see
This is the life's most important key
Learn from oxygen giving generous tree.

Go To Planetarium

Don't see eclipse with necked eye
With proper fillers you can try
Necked eyes will become dry
Your vision may forever fly
Better, during eclipse remain shy
If you are curious, go to planetarium
There you will learn many things premium
Thank God, people can't harm the sun
Man would have destroyed it for fun
To save sun we don't need symbolic run.

Father's Day

Don't think father is big brother
He is always the best friend rather
He also loves his children like mother
Father, mother take care of you together
It is his responsibility to save you in danger
Father is always rational and kind
A mentor like him no where you can find
But for your future he doesn't follow you blind
If father scold you, no need to keep in mind
On Father's Day memories with him rewind.

Be Grateful

In moment of joy, we forget to be grateful
For long time achievement it is harmful
Ignoring the supporting hand is shameful
If you forget your friends being cheerful
One day your eyes may become tearful
For every small support, help say thank you
You will get many reliable good friends new
Gratefulness will make acceptable your view
In society, your critics will be limited few
Grateful people shine like mountain dew.

Friends Are Also Teacher

Friends are also good teacher
They teach many things better
Everything you can't ask mother
Many things you afraid to ask father
Friends try to give all that answer
Friends teach us love, hate and joy
We learn from them to play with toy
With friend's advice we become boy
Football, cricket and counter strike
From friends we learn how to ride bike.

Learning

Learning is needed for earning
You have money for food buying
Learning also make people cunning
In the journey you can take turning
Rebuild your house even after burning
Learning shows you the path of knowledge
Discipline, punctuality you acknowledge
Learning gives you positive attitude
In life you will never become destitute
Learning helps you to climb high altitude.

Man Is Pushed Back

The tree has welcomed the sun
It is dancing in wind with same fun
The squirrel as usual with his run
Crows are crying for morning bun
The dogs are waiting for their turn
Forbidden is only human crowd
In the park man is now without proud
They are not allowed to sing loud
No one knows why man is pushed back
Can man soon be able to go to track?

Sleep

Sleep is always sweet
We are free from tweet
All anxiety, tensions quit
No need to peel any fruit
We are on the calm route
Sleep gives sweet dream
We can eat free cream
Comfort of sleep invaluable
Day sleep is also comfortable
Without sleep, life is miserable.

Welcome To Garden

Welcome to the garden
Throw away your burden
You will get back your rhythm
God is waiting as Phantom
Corona will lose his fiefdom
Fresh air is waiting for you
Touch with feet morning dew
The day will come as new
You will enjoy the beautiful view
Our old lifestyle let us renew.

Behind The Naughty Smile

Behind the naughty smile
There is darkness hostile
May break your heart fragile
You will be forced to face trial
Before you kiss, think for a while
Behind every rose there is thorn
With thorn only roses born
Try to touch, thorn will blow horn
Your hands will become worn
In your plight no one will mourn.

Transmission

Sometimes a natural process transmission
It doesn't need anyone's permission
Sometimes it needed scientific solution
Electromagnetic waves need amplification
Transmission always do not give satisfaction
Transmission can be good or evil
Transmission of diseases is devil
Without transmission nothing will change
Transmission process human has to manage
To change its path, we need brain and courage.

Love Is Blind

Love is always blind
Every heart you can find
Society it can bind
It is state of the mind
With loved one has you dined?
Love is without boundary
But it must be voluntary
If one party is passive
Love will be expensive
Yet it is like drugs sedative.

Dalai Lama

The modern-day mascot of peace
For better new world he has the keys
Everywhere he planted brotherhood trees
His motherland is still under seize
Will Tibet ever see freedom breeze?
All over world he distributed light
But for his cause with arms never fight
His principle is, nonviolence is right
Bravely facing the Chinese army's might
One day there will be end to Tibetans plight.

Why Me?

When we hit jackpot, we never ask why me
In trouble and pain, we always blame Thee
In good days we forget to pray and see
We never think to thank our friend tree
Everything in the world we want to get free
For our happiness we hope God is bound
But in celebration to him we turn around
We are busy with music and loud sound
In distress we feel lonely and ask why me?
Pray to God to immediately send the key.

Salute The Indian Hero

Salute the Indian hero
Express gratitude and sorrow
They died for our tomorrow
Their own life became narrow
Will remain forever in time's arrow;
They sacrificed their life
Left their children and wife
Bravely faced terrorists' knife
When life is fulfilling and rife
Left for heavenly abode before ripe.

Marriage

Beautiful lady who care
Emotions she share
To face danger she dare
Companion like her rare
To save family always aware;
In life wife is the best companion
To make a home she is champion
Some people may have different opinion
But living together is not the solution
Institution of marriage need no dilution.

Wife

Beautiful lady with naughty smile
Always loves makeup and style
But mood is very, very fragile
Any moment can become hostile
Better to follow her profile;
Very difficult to know her mind
Husband's fault she can easily find
Yet on the pay day she is very kind
Undoubtedly, she is the home maker
When she is in vacation we suffer.

Regret

Don't waste time in regret
Fix your next day's target
Work for your future basket
Sale your produce in market
Success will blow your trumpet
Do regret only to correct mistake
Not to repeat, measures you take
Regret should not be false or fake
Regret is not for backtrack
It is for better solution and retake.

I Don't Want A Life Living On Pill

I don't want a life living on pill
One day slow poison will kill
I want life full of joy and thrill
Want to fly and climb tall hill
I have the capacity to pay bill;
Don't want a life that is stand still
Dislike the advices of rumour mill
Want to avoid doctors paid grill
It is not enjoyable to live more as ill
Want a life which my mind loves to fill.

No One Remain Young Forever

When you are at the top
Try to hang on with rope
Any moment God may drop
You may go down the slope
Falling down you must cope;
You may not be on top for long
To face challenges be strong
Your pride may be proved wrong
Life moves up down like ping pong
Remember, whole life no one remain young.

When A Puzzle We Can't Solve

When a puzzle we can't solve
In the name of God we dissolve
Inside a circle our thinking revolve
New approach stop to evolve
But for solution throw away the glove;
God should not limit the thinking process
In the name of old text don't be obsess
The outdated religion will stop progress
Don't allow mind's horizon to recess
Allow new thinking and fresh air to ingress.

Whom Should We Blame?

How far will go the death toll?
How long will remain close mall?
How many times will be lockdown call?
How much jobs will quickly fall?
Things are changing like moving ball;
The situation is like a fast football game
Suddenly the best player became lame
Defeat will push them towards shame
With all efforts they are trying to tame
Result less game, whom should we blame?

No Point For The Past To Regret

The dark nights I want to forget
No point now for the past to regret
All along the journey was toughest
The path to the shore was longest
But enough experience I could harvest;
To forget the bad days is always better
The tough journey taught life's grammar
Avoiding mistakes to move is smarter
Walking on right track makes life merrier
With determination I can cross any barrier.

I Pray For Your Good Health

I pray for your good health
For seniors health is wealth,
If you are free from diabetes
Your money will not be wastes,
If your blood pressure is perfect
Your life span will not subtract,
If you are not suffering in acidity
Bold is your digestive ability,
In the morning if you bowl is clear
You are healthy, O my senior dear
Corona will continue to flow
But good health will allow you to glow.

The Human Civilization Has Resilience

The human civilization has resilience
It grows in the history through persistence
The character of mankind is perseverance
To biggest threat it can give resistance
Epidemics are always a temporary hindrance;
The empire will again strike back and bloom
Soon there will be sunshine and go away the gloom
Human genes are the fittest one to survive
No sooner the economy and civilization will revive
In better atmosphere people will move out for drive.

Human Civilization Will Not Accept Defeat

Human civilization will not accept defeat
As usual rise after fall it will repeat
Plague, Spanish flu, world war couldn't stop
To destroy civilization the Covid19 will flop
Soon civilization will again rise to the top;
The progress of mankind is not a cakewalk
Many times on the road it had badly stuck
Yet with courage it always rises from ashes
The civilization will not stuck in the bushes
It will overcome problem and continue progress.

Salute Mothers On Mother's Day

There can be a mother without a father
There can't be a father without a mother
Don't think about having sister or brother
Maternity is the truth always to remember
Fraternity is social acceptance rather;
The cruelty of war made patriarch society
But mother continues to lead the polity
Still bear the pain of motherhood with humility
Mothers are the torchbearers of human community
Salute mothers on Mother's Day for their dignity.

Sometimes We Become Lonely Sailor

Sometimes to hide our failure
We become a lonely sailor
Sail our ship of life to mid sea
So that vastness of world we can see
Our existence is smaller than a bee;
Sometimes we are forced to hide
So that we can make our horizon wide
The pride, glory all are momentary
We have to leave this world in solitary
Ego, greed, hate in our life all are mockery.

Might Is Always Not Right

I am always right
It will push to fight
You may have might
Yet will come night
Your position will be tight;
Better you see the light
Navigate your flight
If you are wrong lower height
You can see the world bright
Might is always not right.

Crazy People

If you are crazy
You are not lazy
You only choose
But always busy
Sometimes vision hazy;
Crazy people are not mad
For days don't go to bed
For their dream busy head
In failure never become red
Will not give up till he is dead.

I Am No More Hero

Nothing left in the fridge
No money to pay electricity fees
So, enjoying morning breeze
Remembering taste of cheese
Let hunger subside and decrease;
Lockdown made bank balance zero
In friends circle I am no more hero
So playing my guitar like emperor Nero
Waiting for prediction of astrologer Cheerio
No one knows what will be future of Euro.

Misery Of The Poor

To save life, they left city
Barefoot and thirsty
No money, no resource
Moving to home is the course
Know well, home is not bed of rose;
Walked hundreds of miles
On their faces no smiles
In hot summer life is fragile
Roadside policemen are hostile
The misery of poor will only pile.

Eat Without Mouth

Eat now without mouth
Defecate without sound
Remember world is round
Food poor will not found
To return home they are bound;
Without labour food will not grow
The economic growth will be slow
Supply chain will not smoothly flow
For food people will stand in row
To economy stay in home is a blow.

Poetry Is Free Flow

What is poetry still I can't define
But within boundary it is not confine
It's aroma is better than the best wine
Mother of all literature always shine
I love my poems and they are mine;
No one can write a poem, it is free flow
If you try to compose it will come too slow
The standard of the poem will be very low
In the world of poetry it will never glow
If we try to define poetry it will be hollow.

Think Global Act Local

Man, always forgets, that man is mortal
So efforts are maximum to become global
But basically man are animals rural
Better be satisfied remaining local
Only make your Facebook, Twitter vocal;
Few graveyards are known to be global
Everyone in world can't build Taj Mahal
Yet in your area you can become social
Your attention for success will be focal
Message of Corona is 'think global act local'.

Only For Human Situation Is Critical

The world is moving as usual

To nature everything is casual
We are forced not to be social
Only for human situation is critical
It is not time to play game political;
To become self-sufficient be practical
Try to produce every food item local
In spreading self-reliance be vocal
For the time being forgot to be global
Live with nature and now become rural.

For Better Life People Migrate

For better life people migrate
To earn more is the target
But motherland never forget
Sometimes they also regret
In world they are largest brigade;
To migrant many nations are wicked
During danger their problems cascade
Remember whom they forgot for decade
To return home many places stampede
Citizenship acts will now be differently made.

March Ahead

March ahead, march ahead
We must earn our bread
Otherwise we will be dead
Staying home will not feed
Between the lines please read;
Throw away caste and creed
Forget about luxury and greed
People have to fulfil the need
Sleeping on bed is bad indeed
Plough for spreading wheat seed.

Electricity Can't Be Seen

Ohms law is easy
Kirchhoff's law is messy
Coulomb's law is hazy
Faraday's law is lazy
Gauss's law is drowsy;
Electricity can't be seen
Power factor is lean
To improve it be keen
Watt's law depicts power
No power without tower.

Electrical Is At Top

If electricity stop
Ventilators will flop
Electrical is at top
They are invisible soap
But getting lollipop;
Like air, water; electricity is must
Without electricity people will bite dust
Now in society doctors, nurses are hero
For police also people express sorrow
To electrical people's attitude is narrow.

Migrant Workers

Try to understand migrants' plight
In their name politics is now not right
Condition of labourers are really tight
Their future is not at all very bright
Society together must show them light;
On road labourers are in pathetic condition
Doing politics in such matter is our tradition
In society no one should infuse social pollution
Insult to migrants is inhuman and rights violation
All political parties of India please find a solution.

Come Out Smiling

Forgetting death come out smiling
To face danger come out dancing
Always maintain social distancing
Within family don't avoid soliciting
Avoid only gatherings in socialising;
Come out to see the new horizon
In future life make required provision
Forget many old custom and tradition
Very soon mankind will see solution
Life will flourish with new substitution.

Human Supremacy Nullified

Environment is beautified
Traffic movement simplified
Food habits are rectified
Staying at home specified
Nature's act can be justified;
Before nature animals testified
Air, water, jungle all are purified
Man's unethical behaviour verified
Human supremacy is nullified
All our activities should be dignified.

Budget

Indian budget is gambling of monsoon
Corona overcast everything so soon
Suddenly sun sets in the mid noon
No one knows when will see full moon
Life of finance minister is now a toon;
No one can predict even for next month
No remedy from the invisible Corona wrath
No one can tell how long will stay on earth
Remedy is to find alternate budgeting path
Soon economies will see Corona bloodbath.

Don't Demotivate Frontline Warrior

Don't demotivate frontline warrior
They are our survival barrier
Let's try to keep them merrier
To save our life they may become carrier
Remember to face diseases is their career;
Doctors, nurses and other hospital staff
In their works they can't now give you bluff
Seeing their protective kits don't laugh
Without wearing will not realise how much tough
To medical workers be polite and kind not rough.

Whom To Be Saluted?

Environment has become less polluted
For this whom to be saluted?
Though our lives are commuted
The achievement should not be diluted
This has happened because nature wanted;
We must now engineer balanced development
In areas of animal kingdom no need of our settlement
Environment friendly technology we must implement
To the future generation it will be complement
Mother nature will give to it positive supplement.

What Next?

What is next
SMS me text
I will forward
You will get award
No monetary reward;
Do your own assumption
Do permutation, combination
To be winner give good solution
Award will be small distinction
You will become an institution.

Night Is Now Night

Day is now day
Night is night
To make night bright
Now we don't fight
This is approach right;
More use of natural light
Consumption of fuel is tight
Emission of carbon is not at height
Night clubs and pubs are quite
In nest animal faces less plight.

Newspapers Are In Trouble

Newspapers are in trouble
Book readers become double
Sales has not increased multiple
E-book may be reason probable
Buy also hard copy, request humble;
Printed book has may advantage
You can easily fold a page
Quickly start and stop at any stage
Touching and holding we feel amaze
For reading books let's create craze.

VC (Video Conferencing)

Video conferencing is better than travel
It has saved lot of carbon emitting fuel
No need of secret conversations in dual
Bosses can't fire suddenly becoming cruel
Lesser responsibility as discussed in plural;
Being time bound, there is less debate
You can't tell you are busy and so late
Things on record, nothing you can forget
If you give false statement, have to regret
No one can exaggerate his actual target.

Don't Be Afraid

Don't be afraid to fight
To face bravely is right
Fight with your all might
Fasten your belt tight
Soon we will see light;
Don't be tired of struggle
Otherwise you face trouble
Do not allow enemy to smuggle
With hot water always do gurgle
Pray to the God and be humble.

He Who Afraid Is Dead

He who afraid of fighting is dead
Only for the fittest the world is made
Coward will die sleeping on the bed
Before facing enemy bowed their head
Courageous are not afraid to see blood red;
Don't accept defeat till the last moment
There may be upside down in the event
Ignore negative people's bad comment
Listening to them never become dormant
Till death, defeat is not event permanent.

How To Save Economy?

How to save economy is million dollar question
There is no readymade or quick fix solution
Many economies has already gone in hibernation
All nations now have to go for serious interaction
To implement any measure, need is people's participation;
Dead people will never come back, very sad
But due to poverty thousands will become mad
The conditions of working class is now very bad
To lift family burden incapable now many dad
Nobody knows when the world will come out of red?

Life And Economy Both Are In Danger

Cut your coat according to your cloth
In danger life and economy both
Even earning one penny has worth
For social distancing take a oath
Every penny counts is now truth;
Economy may reach the rock bottom
To save economy there is no Phantom
So never spend money in random
Good new of economy will come seldom
The whole world is now Corona's fiefdom.

No Need To Make Life Slow

Even if you bend, cloud will not go
So, no need for us to bow
As usual cloud will flow
It can't give us any blow
No need to make life slow;
After rain sunshine will certainly come
Though cloud caused disruption some
The dark cloud never stays long
So, no need to bend, be strong
If you stop moving, it will be wrong.

New Generation, Don't Worry

New generation don't worry
With ease face the query
Soon, virus will say sorry
Back will be all old glory
Again you will become merry;
The pause you face is temporary
Work now in your own territory
Place your idea on right trajectory
Store your innovation in inventory
We will praise your success story.

Body Language

Body language is now more important
Everywhere tongue is no more omnipotent
Now you have to communicate from distant
For social distancing we have commitment
So body language become very pertinent;
Body language can express better than words
You can't stop vehicle shouting on roads
For acceptance sufficient is smiling nods
To scold, through gesture can give pose odds
Now to communicate tongue need not take all loads.

Middle Class Has Become Lonely

Middle class has become lonely
Poor people penniless coolly
They accepted the enemy calmly
So roaming around for food silently
Poor has power to face situation bravely;
Rich people are not worried for money
In their hives they stored enough honey
Middle class is worried for heavy tax
So, without work in home they can't relax
The condition of middle class is like latex.

Swab Test

To prevent Corona, necessity is swab test
Quickly knowing about Corona, it is best
Detecting the virus is like killing of pest
Once detected, Corona can be put to rest
Though man is pushed to quarantine nest
Against Corona antibiotics are toothless
So, Corona is becoming day by day ruthless
How to destroy it scientists are clueless
Swab test is now the best preventive way
Do your swab test today, you need not pay.

Enemy Of Poor

Corona is enemy of the poor
Closed their livelihood door
Destroyed food grain store
Rich is also safe any more
Let us stop the naughty whore
The fight against Corona is simple
Distance to be maintained by people
Corona will not be able to dribble
Hugging unknown is horrible
To prevent mask, hand wash is reliable.

We Are Helpless

We are now helpless creature
Worried for my children's future
Schools, colleges are closed down
Activities are standstill at lockdown
The family can't roam in the town
Forced imprisonment is doing harm
On their faces, there is no charm
Children's attitude is now not warm
In home they are tired of virtual swims
We are passing days at nature's whims.

The Virtual World

The virtual world has engulfed our life
People are also staying with virtual wife
Children play in the virtual playground
Their attitude will be different it is bound
Life of people will be within a circle round
Virtual life is not the reality of the world
You can't feel the Mount Everest's cold
Virtual world will not teach how to climb
During danger people will become dumb
Virtually, you can't fertilize a woman's womb.

Fear Of Death

Fear of death is terrible
Life in world is now horrible
To hug the best friend not reliable
Infection of Covid19 is possible
Staying inside home is desirable
Covid19 is making our life miserable
Day by day it is becoming intolerable
Will it become an enemy formidable?
If we don't fear death, we are not vulnerable
To defeat Covid19 with courage struggle.

Epidemic

Epidemic is part of human story
But man, always forgets the history
Because too short is public memory
It is not like disease of coronary
Which is always in society to worry
Epidemics are very dangerous
In the epicentre it is ferocious
Initially people remain curious
Seeing death becomes serious
Then vaccine become precious.

World Is Burning

World is burning
People are crying
China is shining
Kits are supplying
Money is earning;
China is lying
They are playing
Truth is missing
Death is increasing
Trump is bullying;
Death is coming
People are dying
Bodies are lying
Vaccine not finding
Nations are praying.

Life Has Become Dull

Life has become dull
Infront is Corona wall
Brain static inside skull
Activities in state of lull
Boredom in life is full
Corona can't make us fool
The wall we must pull
To do it let's work cool
We have to invent tool
Soon man will again rule.

Don't Worry, Be Happy

Soon everything will be fine
In restaurants we will dine
Bars and pubs will sale wine
We can drink with tasty swine
People will cultivate good vine
For time being we are now mime
We are in the world for limited time
Let us make it a melodious rhyme
Avoid all types of violence and crime
To make world Corona free is duty prime.

Good News Coming Soon

We are waiting for the good news
People will write different views
Pharma companies will earn huge
Vaccine will blow Corona's fuse
The virus will not be able to abuse
Challenge of the virus may be tall
But soon from the top it will fall
Corona will remain as a virus small
Even children will kick it like a ball
Forever the virus will lose fame and hall.

Astrology

Astrology is not a science
It is ostrich mentality blind
To falsehood don't be kind
Faith in it remove from mind
Positivity you will easily find
Astrology is against uncertainty
To change future, it is not immunity
No good it can do to the humanity
Only for fun, astrology has utility
Scientific mind knows its futility.

Religion Need Substitution

Religion failed to remove racism
Religion failed to stop fascism
Religion failed to eradicate caste
Religion failed to control human lust
Religion failed to prevent nuclear blast
Religion encourages gender inequality
Religion promotes jihad and brutality
Religion is never against superstition
Religion showed blind eye to prostitution
Religion now needs better substitution.

Politics

Politics decide nation's future
It is part of our social culture
Don't hate politics as vulture
Our children's future will rupture
Without politics democracy will puncture
Politics is always necessary evil
Don't avoid it considering devil
Through voting, you take part little
Otherwise, bad people will rule and kill
Take part in politics, do mental drill.

Religion And Politics

Religion is the opium of masses
But politics is everything's bases
For power and money everyone races
Study Ramayana, Mahabharata cases
You will realise politics is root causes
Religion and politics two sides of the coin
Combining both politicians try to gain
To bribe for return religion also train
But to grab power mission always main
In human civilization both are in chain.

Don't Hate Sinner

Jesus said 'hate the sin, not the sinner'
For whole world it is a teaching better
For better world its implication is greater
It must be implemented in spirit and letter
Life in world will be happy and merrier
Hate Brahminical culture, not the Brahmin
Indian polity the caste system is denting
De-facto discrimination the system is promoting
So many rituals in religion not suitable in modern time
If we pray God through honest good work that is fine.

Pain

No pain no gain
Pain and gain are in chain
Hard work is main
To accept failure train
Umbrella required in rain
Some work will go to drain
Some efforts will be in vain
Control pain using the brain
The ultimate goal is main
The road to success full of pain.

Cave Man

Suddenly we are forced to be cave man
Inside home caged all football loving fan
Roaming outside for long is totally ban
Our home is now quarantine Eden
We can't do party now even with ten
Like cave man, our only goal is food
More we stay inside home is good
Our lives are in danger from invisible tiny
For safety cave man took shelter in cave is irony
But modern man faced to become cave man is funny.

Baba Ramdev

He popularised yoga among masses
In television also take yoga classes
For yoga Ramdev is real ambassador
To promote better health, he is coordinator
In marketing products also superior
Without big stars he can sale his product
So, in selling advertising cost he can deduct
In politics also he has enviable qualities
To succeed in business, it is requisites
Will his Corona medicine be ventilators substitutes?

Someone May Be Rowdy

Morning may be cloudy
Someone may be rowdy
You may not stand proudly
Yet smile and laugh loudly
Sun will come soon undoubtedly
Morning may not be beautiful
But move forward being cheerful
The whole day will not be harmful
Only movement should be careful
End of the day, you will see plentiful.

Failure And Suicide

Failure has nothing to do with suicide
It is only one's attitude that decide
All great people have died before success
Through failure only success they access
To kill one's own life failure never teaches
Failures will come and failures will go
But it will help your experience to grow
More experience means more perfection
Soon you will do your job with satisfaction
Failure will not remain as factor of limitation.

Sour To Sweet Always Matter

Sour mango becomes sweet
Bad company immediately quit
False matters never tweet
In mind negativity should not weed
Changing attitude be a new breed
In stomach bitter pill no more bitter
To change attitude use mind's filter
Good messages spread through Twitter
Enlarge your horizon to think greater
Changing sour to sweet always matter.

Toe To Top

Take care from toe to top
Otherwise, task will flop
Dirty things quickly mop
Avoid falling on the slope
Tension you have to cope
With determination gallop
Don't lose because of dope
Best results always hope
Consistency tie with rope
With failure never elope.

Truth Is Always Truth

Truth is truth irrespective of religious belief
During epidemic prayer can't give you relief
Many age-old beliefs proved to be wrong
But truth is always true and remain strong
If truth hurts religious sentiment, sing a song
Religious texts are not verified by standard norms
So many things in religious texts are harmful worms
Your beliefs may sometimes be hurt by necked truth
But remember, truth most of the times are ruth
Belief alone can't save forever your religion's booth.

We Pray Sun And Moon

We pray the sun, because it gives light
We pray Moon, because in night it is bright
But to pray for our earth, we always fight
To destroy mother earth, we think is right
Corona has now made our position tight;
Sun and Moon don't need our protection
So, to pray them we have big attraction
Mother earth seriously need our attention
But every moment we are doing humiliation
To save mother earth need new solution.

Saturday Night Fever

Saturday night fever is missing
In home we are in forced hiding
Every weekend depression is rising
Our enthusiasm for party is dying
On Sunday also no more roaming
Party, get together are dangerous
Because in the air there is virus
We are wasting our time precious
To save life we must be serious
The Covid19 is still going furious.

Bad Potato

It is dangerous even one rotten potato
To destroy others is always it's motto
Throw away it immediately from basket
Before it starts to sale destruction ticket
Bad potato can spread odour like cricket
One naughty man can destroy a society
To spread bad things people are plenty
People love to carry rumour in their kitty
Identify the rotten potato in your vicinity
To have a better society will be reality.

Religion Is Deep Rooted

Religious beliefs are very deep rooted
From generation to generation imported
With society for thousands of years integrated
Religion and culture difficult to be differentiated
Throughout the whole world beliefs has migrated;
The older generations never allow reform
With their grandfather they always conform
No one is allowed to modify the deform
Thus, religion became opium for masses
But religion failed to eradicate racism and classes.

Peace

Peace is a state of mind
In loneliness you can find
To everyone always be kind
In search of peace don't be blind
Peace is sitting just behind
Every human love peace
But for mistake they miss
It remains like a flying kiss
A never eaten delicious dish
Open your mind, see the bliss.

Career And Opportunity

You may fail in hundred metres stint
In four hundred you are queen of sprint
Through practice in marathon, you can mint
Never allow failure to keep imprint
Practice gives perfection is the hint
If you fail to shine in running track
Long jump, high jump is in the back
In pole vault or javelin, you may not lack
In life and career there is no guarantee
But world is full of hurdles and opportunity.

Career And Life

Career should not be a barrier
For better life we need career
But it is more important to be merrier
Chase your dreams to be happier
You can't be happy being money chaser
To chase career don't lost in desert
Better compose music to become Mozart
If you are in wrong track better to restart
Remember career is only life's small part
Chasing career alone don't make life dirt.

We Are Good In Corruption

We the Indian are good in corruption
If our mentality is this there is no solution
Everyone wants encashment of chance
Along with people Government also dance
Black marketing opportunity no one denounce
We like to extort money from the poorest
But against corruption never unitedly protest
People will indulge in corruption in chance slightest
Lockdown in Assam used by all to mint quick money
Assamese people also consider corruption as honey.

Luxury Cruise

Life is now passing of day
Every morning comes ray
But we are standstill at bay
Employer not willing to pay
No one is listening to our say
Golden eggs now we can't lay
On board no one willing to play
We are at one place from May
O' Lord show us light and way
Save us from this luxurious tray.

Street Vendor

From city many people vanished
Financially forever they are finished
Street vendors has now diminished
They don't have showroom furnished
Their image Corona has tarnished
The footpath sellers are now hard hit
Two times meals they could not meet
With them economy is playing bullshit
These poor vendors no one likes to greet
Towards them fate has very badly treat.

Happiness Is Like Morning Dew

Happiness is like morning dew
It is enjoyed by selected few
Every day it comes being new
To go back again you can't rew
To be happy many do not knew
Happiness is life's contemporary
You can find it even in solitary
It follows only your rule and directory
For happiness you are your own Notary
You can't invite happiness like dignitary.

Failed Marriages

Now a days many marriages fail
For long together husband-wife can't sail
In small accident the train forced to derail
They can't reconcile even through mail
But divorce no one in the family hail
Intolerance is the most important reason
They wish to have spring in all the season
Ego injects in mind negativity and poison
Both will try to impose his forced solution
Relationships pushed to ultimate dilution.

Cyber Crime

Cyber-crime may be virtual
But pain inflicted is actual
Virtual crime is also cruel
Rumours add to it fuel
The virtual crime affects are duel
Cyber criminals difficult to detect
Sometimes far reaching their effect
In first instance their proposal is reject
Otherwise, you bank balance will subtract
In doing fraud cyber criminals are perfect.

What My Poems Mean

My poems mean the spirit of life
It means love is the cutting knife
My poems mean mankind will strive
For better new world people always drive
Only a value-based world can survive
My poems mean love all hate none
Through brotherhood good is done
My poems mean nature is cute and fine
Do good to all creatures and enjoy wine
It means beautiful world and life is mine.

Simplicity

Simplify your own life
You can't simplify wife,
Simplicity is greatness
To simplify others madness
Within self, simplicity harness
Simplicity is not blindness
Nor it is looseness
Rather it is kindness
It is heart's softness
It represents highness.

Defeat Is Never Final

Sometimes we got defeated
Our task remains in completed
Prayer to almighty not answered
Yet don't accept defeat and move on
Soon God will come to help his son
Defeat is never final till our death
Every forward move count and worth
The game may be tough and too short
Weather may be hostile and very hot
Score the winning goal in the last shot.

Good Morning

In the morning try to feel good
The whole day better will be mood
You will not behave anyone rude
Morning shows the day we all know
If we start with good, positivity will flow
When we start the game with positive mind
In the end of the day, victory we will find
Even to the toughest ball we can hit blind
Start the day with smile and good morning
To negativity of mind, it is the first warning.

Gravity

Gravity don't allow us to fly away
But flights can fly in runway
Birds can easily overcome
Yet, to the sky we can't jump
To fly a balloon also need pump
Against gravity we have to work every moment
Gravity is the balancing force silent
But defying gravity volcanoes are violent
Without gravity life in world is impossible
Gravity is also a powerful God invisible.

No One Will Share Your Pain

If you think someone will share your pain
You must be a fool
Your pain will never cool
To reduce use your own tool
You have to swim yourself in pool
With selfish people world is full
Selfishness is the survival rule
To be safe in winter use better wool
If you fall in sick no one will pull
To survive in painful world, be a strong bull.

The Dust

The tiny minute particle
It can tell earth's Chronicle
Without it land mass not feasible
Together they made continent possible
The existence of minute particle is viable
You be small like a tiny dust
But even than you can survive and last
The tiny things can fly easily and fast
No weather force you to change to rust
You never carry baggage of the past.

Use Your Money

Everyone works for money
Money can buy sweet honey
Comfortable become journey
With best coach you win tourney
You are dead, if you are without penny
Money is the converted form of work
It has no use if you earn simply to stock
The associated value of work, you block
Money will lose value, for long if you lock
Use your money in the night club and rock.

Thoughts

Thoughts are powerful
Because it creates action
It always pushes us to motion
Thoughts also create emotion
To our problems thought give solution
Thoughts make human better animal
So, never allow your thought to be cruel
For revenge, to your thought don't add fuel
Your thought process should work for well
In the mind, bad thoughts don't allow to swell.

India-China Standoff

India-China standoff
For Pakistan it is lollipop
Peace in region shall flop
Economic activity will stop
Settlement everyone hope
War is not good for both nation
Better is amicable solution
Status quo will reduce tension
Both nations need more discussion
To people war will bring destruction.

Snake

All snakes are not poisonous
They are always not dangerous
But fear on human minds marvellous
To kill them people become furious
Now to save snakes let's be serious
For biodiversity snakes are necessary
They always live in their own territory
Rodents and insects are their food
In balancing these, snakes are good
Behaviour of man makes snakes rude.

Don't Carry Painful Burden

Don't carry painful burden of past
To move forward discarding it must
Otherwise, your thoughts will rust
Every moment present will bite dust
The pain will bring your end fast
Pain of past are like dirty garbage
Throw them and home nicely manage
There is nothing in it for salvage
They will only make environment savage
The pain of past is also dirty luggage.

China, Enjoy Your Own Territory

China should stop expansionist attitude
Chinese people are present in all latitude
People are important than barren land
This is time for Chinese leaders to amend
Otherwise, they will lose all their friend
China already occupying a large territory
For grabbing others land they shouldn't hurry
The whole world they are making worry
For hurting others, they should say sorry
Being friends with neighbour will be big lottery.

Decision Making

Use your brain to analyse
Listen to heart to finalize
Attitude necessary to modernize
Apply experience to merchandise
Wisdom necessary to synchronise
Decision making is always tough
But decision should not be rough
It should not be eyewash or baked half
Decision should not also be bluff
It should always be best and fair enough.

Broker

Brokers are necessary for land deal
Many brokers digital medium kill
To get a rented house they are bitter pill
Commission from both party they steal
Sock market is brokers mid-day meal
Without broker Indian marriage difficult
To get contract they can give result
Broker joins the gap between two sides
In society many decisions broker decides
To fix a deal, to both parties' broker lies.

China Is Destabilising World

China has destabilized world peace
Even our girlfriend now we can't kiss
The feeling of globalization we miss
The great wall will not be able to save
Against them in the world there is wave
China is trying to show their brave face
But this time they will not win the race
Together all nations will break their base
To defuse tensions China is doing less
In international forum they will lose all case.

No One Can Stop Time

No one can stop change
But his own time he can manage
Every moment brain remains engage
In better thinking try to arrange
If you don't accept change, you are strange
Even if you remain asleep, change will come
Change in your appearance will be done
You will never get back the time that has gone
Those who try to resist change are fool
Accept change, adjust with it and be cool.

Green

Let us make the world green
For oxygen mankind is keen
Everywhere pollution is seen
To love greenery train teen
In world green should be seen
Green will give us food security
To plant tree everyone's duty
The colour of green has beauty
Ever green things are not naughty
He who destroy green is guilty.

Luck

Hard working people favoured by luck
Yet sometimes the best player score duck
Someone may hit you with his truck
With half done job you may stuck
Failure many a times called bad luck
You may lose your hard-earned buck
But your fortune no one can suck
Your spirit to work, no one can pluck
Hard worker will work even in dark
Because other side of the coin is luck.

Obedience

Obedience is good quality for student
To the teachers one should be obedient
Obedience encourages to be prudent
For discipline also, obedience pertinent
Obedience helps you for containment
Obedient people are gentle and polite
Their behaviour is also always elite
Working with obedient, we feel delight
Punctuality is obedience's highlight
In armed forces obedience is always right.

Teacher Teaches

Teachers teaches
Students catches
Exam is matches
Upward reaches
Goes out batches
Parents' wishes
Teachers preaches
Students misses
Play in beaches
Sometimes kisses.

Lecture

Lecture, lecture and lecture
Lectures are no more pleasure
They are not inspiring new venture
For nation not creating treasure
Lecture is not a good culture
Corona made economy to puncture
Lockdown is doing cruel torture
We need now new economic structure
More investment needed in agriculture
Poor people can't withstand more pressure.

Dependency

Dependency is not a good habit
You will become weak like a rabbit
For your work don't depend on other
Peace of mind you will lose rather
Happiness will close its shutter
Dependency will dilute your initiative
In learning, you will not be attentive
Development of mind will not be progressive
In every walk of life, you will remain submissive
Your life will become fearful and passive.

Innovation

Think out of the box
Sometimes chase fox
But don't tell hoax
Be strong like an ox
Find new variety of cox
Break the black box
Don't bother for pox
Ignore people's vox
Be vigil to hackers dox
Avoid people's NOx.

Age Is Gift Of Time

Age is time's non-returnable gift
But your history you can certainly draft
If you work effectively during the day
In the year end, success will show ray
Dividend and bonus time will again pay
As you gather moss of the time
To utilise it better will be duty prime
Experience will make you champion
You will not need require other's opinion
Time makes us expert on problem solution.

Animal Sacrifice Is Superstition

Sacrificing animal for God is superstition
It is religious intellectual prostitution
Once on human sacrifice had no restriction
Seeing innocents' blood, what will be God's position?
In religion, animal sacrifice needs substitution
All living beings including man created by God
To sacrifice his own creation, God will not give nod
Sacrificing animal to please God is inhuman act
Some vested interests get benefits is the real fact
To stop animal sacrifice for God, humanity should react.

Untold Agony

Untold agony is painful
For mind it is harmful
Sometimes eyes are tearful
To avoid agony, be skilful
Life is precious and beautiful
Agony is creation of mind
In mind, solution in easy to find
To the situation be easy and kind
The past incident doesn't rewind
With positivity new doctrine sign.

Kick

Mother camel gives a kick
The baby stands up from seat
Starts to run on his weak feet
For survival, lethargy must beat
The kick is always igniting hit
In life sometimes kick is required
Otherwise, the skill can't be acquired
The kick can ignite body and mind
For survival, path we can quickly find
The mother camel knows, nature is not kind.

Evil

Negative minds think evil
They slowly become devil
With them bad things prevail
To destroy, they work with will
For petty reason, they can kill
Evil thinking breeds evil people
Bad people are never simple
Their motive is to create trouble
Their own lives also slowly cripple
Under evil pressure, they are bound to buckle.

Today Is The Right Time

Today is the right time to start your project
If you postpone it, time will then reject
Your project will remain as imaginary object
For the examination today start a new subject
Otherwise after exam result sheet will reject
Today is the right time for outing with family
To make it reality, manage your time properly
Return to home from your office timely
The beautiful day like today comes rarely
For better tomorrow, utilise today wisely.

Today Or Never

Today is the best time to propose her
Tomorrow she may move to a city too far
Today is the time to join broken friendship
Tomorrow your friend may help you in hardship
Today is the best time to go to temple and worship
Today will never come back and gone forever
Your beautiful today, with dear one's share
Today is the right time to patch up with estranged wife
Tomorrow it will again change your life
Today is always better than a great tomorrow hype.

All Lives Matter

All lives matter, black or white
Justice must be fair and right
Rule of law should glow bright
For equality of law let us fight
To all, law and order to be tight
No discrimination for colour
Everyone should get his honour
Equality and fair play need of hour
Black, white all is part of the tower
Society must be like internet browser.

Make Democracy Better

When all lives will matter
Democracy will be better
All citizens to be treated equal
Against discrimination, be vocal
Equality of law must be global
Colour discrimination is worst crime
To punish racists, democracy's duty prime
The racism is a crime against humanity
To eradicate racism, show solidarity
Change of mindset will bring parity.

For Better World

Move with courage and confidence
Move ahead with honesty and courage
Integrity, confidence should be luggage
For greed there should not be haulage
Your morality and ethics not for mortgage
Evil thinking in the mind don't encourage
Courage and confidence will give success
Honesty, integrity golden road to progress
Without greed you will never face recess
Your full potential you can freely harness
No one will bother for your race or dress.

Cleanliness

Cleanliness is minds holiness
Cleanliness is day to day business
Cleanliness is also consciousness
Cleanliness is life's vastness
Cleanliness enhances kindness
Clean your home everyday
It will give to your life ray
With positive though clean mind
Your attitude will be honest and kind
Happiness in life you will easily find.

If You Live In Poverty

If you are living in poverty
Convert it to life's liberty
Try, soon to attain puberty
With confidence show solidarity
Make your companion integrity
Poverty can't stop your honesty
You don't have valuable property
You are not going to lose monetary
Honest living should be priority
Freedom of life is your warranty.

Bamboo

Bamboo is known as green good
In markets easily bamboo can be sold
In rural life it is material of household
Matured bamboo is strong and bold
Bamboo houses are beautiful and cold
Biodegradable grass is eco friendly
Bamboo protect environment boldly
Rural economy it strengthens solidly
Delicious recipe is made with bamboo shoot
Bamboo can be easily cultivated with its root.

Give And Take

Approach in the society is give and take
Otherwise, the behaviour of people is fake
You scratch my back; I will scratch your
Even love and smiles are not always pure
For the intention of friends don't be sure
Greed and selfishness now order of the day
How the society will change, no hope of ray
Only the residue of values is surviving
The world has become habitat of cunning
Hope for a better new world diminishing.

The World Is Whole, Perfect And Complete

The world is whole, perfect and complete
Don't think our life is incomplete and little
Though our life is imperfect and brittle
To make it perfect make your life simple
Life is whole, when we are happy couple
We are born and living in the perfect world
So, to make life complete always be bold
Keep all the misery and pain in the cold
The better part of the life continuously unfold
Complete, whole, perfect life glitters like pure gold.

Poverty And Discrimination

Poverty and discrimination
We need a good solution
God failed in their dilution
Economists gave presentation
But solution is still in illusion
Religion must go to back burner
Education should be the front runner
New formula for distribution of wealth
Nation should also take care of health
In poverty there should not be any death.

Master And Slave

We are not master of nature
But we did unabated torture
Destruction become culture
Now our tyres are puncture
Nature is doing us torture
We must now play role of slave
Otherwise, we have to stay in cave
To serve nature we should be brave
Nature will give way if we nicely behave
If we don't change place, we will be in grave.

Pseudo Religious

I dislike pseudo religious
Better is singer melodious
Like people who are conscious
Respect the scientist's genius
Love the company of meritorious
Pseudo religious are fraud and greedy
They deceive poor and the needy
Never they have seen shadow of God
Only for money with people do fraud
When they ask money to show them road.

Woman

Bold and beautiful
Women are dutiful
She is very helpful
Smiling and cheerful
Rarely she is harmful
Though condition is painful
She maybe tearful
But She never act wilful
Beautiful woman plentiful
Gender inequality is shameful.

How To Avoid Depression

To avoid depression
Create your impression
Painting may give satisfaction
Writing book is a solution
Play instrument for dilution
Talk to your friends freely
Play football, cricket coolly
Present your points boldly
Discuss with counsellors boldly
You can control depression firmly.

Healing

Healing is pain pealing
You star good feeling
Healing is germs nailing
Disease starts falling
Attitude helps healing
Positivity needed for killing
Meditation helps sailing
Negativity pushes to boiling
Don't allow others for pulling
Healing will make your smiling.

Blame

If you play the game of blame
Failure you will not be able to tame
In society, you will earn bad name
In the end you will face shame
For success bad is blame game
For your failure don't blame father
For his support thank him rather
For failure, your role is greater
Playing blame game don't be smarter
I am responsible for my failure actually matter.

All Well If Ends Well

All well if ends well
Success stories tell
If defeat people smell
They will raise warning bell
You have to go to hell
No one will remember your effort
With winner people will seek comfort
Defeated warrior no one support
Your good things no one will export
If end product is well, everybody will import.

Surname

Surname is generally hereditary
It is family's bond and solidarity
It is also for someone's identity
To win title in sports positive mentality
Sometimes titles are winner's identity
To win more titles people work hard
Olympic title is life's success card
Winning world cup you can fly like bird
Some titles are only feather in the cap
These titles also enlarge satisfaction map.

Follow Safety Measures Seriously

Take safety measures very seriously
Otherwise, Corona will infect notoriously
It will harm to your lungs dangerously
People will see your condition curiously
Some people are spreading rumours falsely
Covid19 is a real threat to our mankind
Vaccine is not yet scientists could find
The virus may also spread through wind
Till now masks and sanitiser has to bind
Follow safety rules, to neighbour be kind.

Farmers Can't Work From Home

Farmers can't work from home
Consequence what may come
Cultivation is not an indoor activity
To work outside is their day-to-day duty
They produce food for the humanity
Farmer must plough field on time
To saw seed timely is their duty prime
If they wait for Corona, there will be famine
In future people will not get food and wine
Yet in poverty farmers suffer, can't shine.

Farmer's, Please Work Online

Farmers should also work online
After Corona economy will be fine
Free meals everyone will get to dine
In ration shops no need to make line
With alcohol we will enjoy online swine
Misery of farmers under sun will vanish
From home all jobs they will easily finish
With online money their debt will diminish
Their agricultural products will not perish
Forever problems of farmers will diminish.

Season Is Changing As Usual

Nothing has changed in world
Only our lifestyle has become cold
Misery of poor people remain untold
In market quickly vegetables can be sold
A different society forced Corona to unfold
Season is changing as usual with time
The morning sun is also bright and fine
People get same taste while drinking wine
In farms very good is the growth of vine
But time forced to change lifestyle mine.

Faith

Faith is a good prime mover
In life it is your land rover
Long distance you can cover
Faith has amazing power
God's blessings it can shower
Faith in self is the self-confidence
It helps you to work with persistence
You can work in life with substance
Your faith in life is your own ordinance
Good faith in life is best incidence.

We Have Destroyed Elephant's Habitat

We have destroyed elephant's habitat
Yet for long they remain totally silent
To elephant-man conflict, elephant was lenient
To nature's law elephants were always obedient
Man- elephant conflict is now permanent
Elephants have also equal right to life and food
To kill them on flimsy ground by man is not good
This behaviour will force nature to angry mood
Nature will punish mankind with actions rude
Let us work to preserve elephant habitat and wood.

O' My Miser Friend

O' my greedy miser friend
Don't be totally blind
In wealth life can't find
To people be kind
For society give mind
Don't chase mirage
To spend show courage
Lighten your baggage
You will leave all luggage
Charity is better mortgage.

We Must Kill The Bustard Corona

Is surviving from Corona now purpose of life?
Earlier it was quarrelling with beloved wife
Mission, goal, objectives are now only hype
A virtual thinking and failed prototype
An invisible enemy become deadly knife
Hiding our face, we can't move forward
We must throw away this unwanted reward
In life we were looking for different award
But now we are on back foot like coward
To achieve goals, we must kill the bustard.

Purpose Of Life

I asked the apple tree
For what purpose you are living?
The tree smiled and answered
"To give you oxygen and sweet fruit
I give shadow and cool breeze
All living beings are in the same crease "
I asked myself, what is my purpose?
Is it to accumulate wealth and money
Or eat, drink and enjoy beautiful tourney?
The tree opened my eyes
I try to look at life from the skies
The purpose is same as the tree
Because air, water, light and time are free
Our purpose is also to do good to others
The living kingdom is our own brothers.

Love For Children Is A Binding Force

When you abandon your own child
Your heart must be very wild
Whatever may be the reason
For the child it is a treason
The child's mind pushed to prison
Love for children is a binding force
It is mankind's continuity source
Lord Rama abandoned his wife
But his children brighten his life
Abandoning own gene is brutal type.

Faith

Faith is a good prime mover
In life it is your land rover
Long distance you can cover
Faith has amazing power
God's blessings it can shower
Faith in self is the self-confidence
It helps you to work with persistence
You can work in life with substance
Your faith in life is your own ordinance
Good faith in life is best incidence.

Go To Garden And Shout

Is life only for food and sex?
Is government for only to collect tax?
Life is now burning like candle wax
Lifestyle is now like outdated fax
What to gain or lose if days become max?
Initially we have counted the bad days
Now not at all excited to see morning rays
It is uncertain how many months to count
We may have to count years is also in doubt
To reduce frustration, go to garden and shout.

227. Testing time

Testing time of mankind
Humans are determined
Resilience to be pinned
Confidence to be hinged
Writ against virus signed;
Man, never accept defeat
Epidemics may repeat
With vaccine man will treat
Deadly blow antibody will hit
Covid19 will take retreat.

I Am Nothing

In this world I am nothing
So, always try to do something
Life's journey is not only eating
Every stoppage does a meeting
But never do any cheating
Don't waste time sitting or sleeping
Better work to street children teaching
For pleasure do a beautiful painting
Take part in knowledge spreading
One day society will say, you are good thing.

Einstein

Slow and steady wins the race
Einstein was not with beautiful face
He was once denied admission
But great was his imagination
So, he could find problems solution
Matter and energy duality of nature
It continued from creation forever
Simplifying it Einstein changed culture
Relativity is natural thing known to people
With his theory Einstein made it simple.

Block

When your anger rock
Someone you block
Communication you lock
In future you can't talk
This is not good work
Better you ignore him
His words will become dim
To hit you, he will not pin
He will realise his sin
To be friendly he will be keen.

Silver Lining

Always try to look at the silvery line
Even at worst situation you will be fine
You can see the winery in the vine
Attitude add flavour and taste in wine
In silver lining remain top number nine
If you can see silver lining in darkness
Soon you are bound to see big success
Silver lining is the road towards progress
Many people don't see it during distress
Try to notice silver line with kindness.

Nothing Is In Our Hand

Nothing is now in our hand
Sanitiser is our best friend
Washing hand is the trend
Habits we have to amend
Mask is the popular brand
We are washing hands without dart
This proves that we are not smart
A new lifestyle we are forced to start
Only food, medicine needed in our cart
All other things in world seems to be flirt.

What Is God

The mystery of life is God
He lives even with tiny tod
God is the strongest iron rod
To move, universe need his nod
He saves the weaker during odd
God is the duality of energy and matter
Through evolution he is doing world better
For mankind he is considered to be father
He can cage time in the womb like mother
In creating the universe, he is the harbinger.

Grace Of God

Truthfulness, nonviolence and honesty
Along with follow the path of amnesty
You will become good member of society
Above board will be your integrity
No need to follow religious nitty-gritty
When your integrity is above board
Life's journey will be on the smooth road
With religious rituals no need to search God
Good deeds and purity of mind is above all
From the grace of God, you will never fall.

The Cruellest Animal

Man is the cruellest animal
But at the same time, he is social
Killing of pregnant elephant is brutal
Really man is personality of dual
People for animals, please fight the cruel
Man is the only animal, who kills all species
With hundreds logic brutality always justifies
All these activities, hypocrisy of human justifies
Nature will give justice to the weaker genes
Man should realise, through Covid19 what nature means.

Inequalities

Exploitation of women in society is intrinsic
It is deep rooted in society than the Atlantic
To torture female, there are too many fanatic
In the name of religion, they force women to remain static
In society against women equality, too many critics
For generations, women tolerate inequalities
To serve male in life is considered to be their duties
Majority of women prefer to remain as sweeties
More concerned about their dresses and beauties
Even in modern days, women live life of inequalities.

Gender Discrimination

One female is killed every thirteen minute
Their voices, orthodox religions try to mute
Worldwide, discrimination against female is acute
In the eyes of nature, families are nice and cute
But to the female, civilized society is brute
Gender discrimination, some society refute
Yet in modern society also, it is not totally dilute
Some women, as our leaders, we used to depute
Women head of nations, we used to salute
But in overall picture, these are only volute
In some societies, supremacy of male is absolute
Asking for equality, women they prosecute
For misery in the family, women they attribute
Thousands of women are forced to become destitute
We must save young from becoming forced prostitute.

I Am Insignificant

How insignificant, I am in the world, makes me funny
I decided to make my living in the world today sunny
Let us smile, dance together and have some honey
Enjoyable and comfortable will be my remaining journey
For enjoying together, no one need to pay me any money
Our existence in the domain of time is unstable
Why to create unnecessary disputes and trouble
Let us resolve everything today, being humble
Our journey for tomorrow is not certain and measurable
The arrow of time may hit in the midnight, and I buckle.

Hypocrisy

The world is full of people with hypocrisy
Their opinions are always selfish and noisy
Double standards people are truly lousy
For own gains and profits, they are busy
To fulfill own interest, they make situation massy
In life, always be aware of hypocrite people
Their thinking is complex, never simple
Your simple life, they can easily cripple
To deal with them, you must learn how to dribble
Otherwise, in every step, they will create trouble.

I Love Jesus And Buddha

I love Jesus and Buddha most
In religion, they are best host
For mankind they cared utmost
Their teaching is priority topmost
We should make their words glasnost
Love and nonviolence, their core value
To keep mankind together, they are glue
As social changer, their contributions don't devalue
Teachings of Jesus and Buddha needs revalue
Let's make them to keep mankind together superglue.

About the Author

Devajit Bhuyan

DEVAJIT BHUYAN, Engineer, Advocate, Management & Career Consultant, was born at Tezpur, Assam, India, on 1st August, 1961. He completed Bachelor of Engineering (Electrical), from Assam Engineering College and subsequently completed Diploma in Industrial Management, from International Correspondence School, Mumbai, LL.B. from Gauhati University, Diploma in Management from Indira Gandhi Open University, and Certified Energy Auditor Examination from Bureau of Energy Efficiency (BEE), New Delhi. He is also a Fellow of the Institution of Engineers (India). He is having 22 years' experience in Petroleum and Natural Gas Sector and 14 years in education management. He has authored 70 books published by different publishers. To know more about him please visit www.devajitbhuyan.com

www.ingramcontent.com/pod-product-compliance
Lightning Source LLC
LaVergne TN
LVHW091634070526
838199LV00044B/1062